THIS BOOK
BELONGS TO
THE ISLANDERS
AND

....

....

....

First published 2011 by
Mabecron Books
42 Drake Circus
Plymouth
PL4 8AB

Illustrations Rebecca Cobb
Designed by Peter Bennett

Typeset in Baskervlle2 BT
Printed in Singapore

ISBN 978 09564 3502 6

For Olivia Grace

THE
ISLANDERS

HELEN DUNMORE

ILLUSTRATIONS BY REBECCA COBB

Mabecron Books

The train whistled as it puffed round the curve of the track.
'The sea!' shouted Robbie.
There it was, blue and glittering, just the same as last year.

Tamsin was waiting at the station. Suddenly she heard the train's whistle. There was the engine, pulling a long snake of carriages packed with holiday visitors. There was Robbie at the window, waving to her. Tamsin raced along the platform, waving back.

The visitors poured off the train. Robbie's mum and dad lifted their cases down onto the platform.
'You two can carry the twins,' said Robbie's mum.
Tamsin carried Lucy, and Robbie carried Sarah. Little Sam trotted alongside as they all set off for Tamsin's cottage.

Tamsin's mum had baked stargazy pie to welcome them. Everybody told stories about what had happened since last summer, but Tamsin and Robbie couldn't wait to go to the beach.
'Watch the tide,' said Tamsin's mum.

Tamsin and Robbie raced along the cobbled streets, down the slipway and onto the sand. Every year they went to their secret place. It was a small white beach, above the tide-line and hidden by rocks. A little stream trickled across it.

'I 've got a new spade,' said Robbie.
'I've got that bucket we found last year,' said Tamsin.
'We'll start digging tomorrow.'
Tamsin and Robbie were planning to make a secret island.

That night Robbie climbed up the rope ladder to the attic room where he slept. He looked out of the window at the stars and thought about the secret island. Tamsin snuggled down with her cat Demelza on her feet, and dreamed about the hut they would build.

In the morning Tamsin's mum gave them sandwiches and a pasty. Robbie's dad gave them money for fizzy lemonade. Tamsin and Robbie took their bucket and spade and other, secret things that they needed for their island.

Robbie and Tamsin dug a channel for the little stream. They made a dam out of stones and packed sand. Now the island had a lake in the middle of it, brimming and bubbling. They made plants and trees out of seaweed. They collected driftwood along the tide-line, and big stones. Tamsin took out the scissors she had brought from home, and the red skirt she had when she was little. She cut out a flag and tied it to a stick. It was hard to decide where to plant the island's flag.

When it was time for their picnic, Robbie fetched the fizzy lemonade from the rock-pool where it was keeping cold. Robbie kept a bit of sandwich for bait, so he could fish for crabs with his line.

The second day, Tamsin brought an old blanket and some sailcloth her brother gave her before he went to sea. They found three stout bamboo poles in the outhouse, and Robbie bought a ball of twine with his holiday pocket-money.

Tamsin and Robbie stuck the poles deep into the sand, in a triangle. They lashed the tips together with Robbie's twine and then draped the sailcloth over the poles and weighed its hem with heavy stones.

'It's a hut made of wild animal skins,' said Robbie.

Tamsin spread her blanket on the floor. Inside the hut it was dark and secret, but you could open the flap and look out at the bright summer day. Robbie and Tamsin ate their picnic inside their hut, and then they decorated the hut's entrance with shells.

B ut the secret island was not finished. On the third day Tamsin and Robbie dragged
armfuls of oarweed across the rocks. They made a mound of sand at the back of
their island and covered it with oarweed.
'It's called the Wild Interior,' said Tamsin.

Every night Sarah and Lucy slept in Tamsin's brother's bedroom, with Robbie's mum and dad. Sam slept in the slip-room and Robbie lay in his attic and looked at the stars. Demelza purred and dug her claws into the blanket over Tamsin's feet. Tamsin's mum did not dream. She was too tired from cooking for eight people. The money from summer visitors paid for Tamsin's winter coat and shoes.

On the fourth day, Robbie caught six little crabs on his line. A long time ago he had been afraid of picking up crabs, but now he didn't care at all. He made a home for the crabs in a rock-pool. Tamsin made a mermaid out of shells and stones, with seaweed hair.

On the fifth day Tamsin and Robbie had visitors. A seal hauled out on a nearby rock and snoozed in the sun. Two gulls perched on the hut, hoping for scraps. Tamsin gave them bits of sandwich.
'You should be catching fish,' she told them.

Robbie stood on a rock, keeping a look-out. Suddenly he shouted, 'Shark ahoy!' Tamsin shaded her eyes, and in the far distance she saw a fin moving slowly southwards.
'It's a basking shark,' she said.

Later the dolphins came, leaping high out of the water as they travelled past Man's Head.

On the sixth day there was only one day left. Tomorrow was Saturday, and Robbie was going home on the train with all his family.
'I wish I didn't have to go,' said Robbie.
'I wish you could stay here for ever,' said Tamsin.
For ever ... for ever ... said the waves as they swashed and backwashed.
Tamsin and Robbie made a plan.

That evening Tamsin filled a basket with slices of her mum's heavy cake and left-over bread and cheese. She and Robbie went to bed, and waited until everyone was asleep. Robbie climbed down the rope-ladder silently. Tamsin pushed Demelza off her feet, and brought a blanket in case the night was cold. They tiptoed downstairs and out into the moonlit street. Tamsin gave Robbie her brother's old jersey and cap to wear. 'Now you look like a proper islander,' she said.

Robbie and Tamsin hurried to the harbour. Below the steps a little boat with red
sails was waiting. Her name was painted white: The Islander.
'Let's hide in that boat until your train's gone.'
They clambered into the bottom of the boat and snuggled under Tamsin's
blanket. There was just time to eat some heavy cake before they fell asleep.

While they were sleeping the tide began to rise. The boat rocked and the moon grew bright. Tamsin opened her eyes. She shook Robbie's shoulder to wake him. 'Robbie, we're moving!'

The Islander spread her sails and the wind began to blow. The Islander glided past the end of Smeaton's Pier, and then they were sailing out of the harbour, into the swell. But there was no crew on The Islander. She was sailing by herself.

'Do you think she knows where she's going?'

The lights of the town slipped away. They were moving out to sea. The sails filled and The Islander leaped through the waves as the lighthouse beam flashed across the water.

A dolphin sprang up alongside them, then crashed back into the waves. Another dolphin leaped clear of the water, and then another.

'The dolphins know where we're going.'

The boat sailed faster, skimming and plunging on the night sea. Tamsin and Robbie held on tight as the wind streamed through their hair.

Ahead, an island rose out of the sea like a humpback whale. Now The Islander slowed and her sails grew slack. The boat with red sails glided into a bay of white sand and came to rest alongside a battered wooden jetty.

Dawn was breaking. The children gazed around. There was a splendid hut, big enough for ten people to sleep in. There was a stream of clear, sparkling water, with pools deep enough for swimming. There were trees covered with golden apples. Behind the hut a steep hill rose towards a dense, mysterious forest.

'Look!' said Tamsin. 'Is that the Wild Interior?'

'I think so,' said Robbie.'

'It's our secret island, but now everything is real,' said Tamsin.

''We can stay here for ever,' said Robbie. 'I won't ever have to go home.'

T hey picked golden apples off the trees. They swam and dived in the deep pools. They gathered bracken to make beds in the hut.

S hall we explore the Wild Interior?'
'Yes, but what if we get lost?'

Tamsin remembered how Hansel and Gretel dropped pebbles to show their trail. She gathered a handful of white pebbles and they set off to explore the Wild Interior. They crept down narrow paths, pushing aside walls of thick, twisting branches. Birds cried out in warning and the branches twined above their heads.

It was very dark in the Wild Interior. Tamsin dropped her pebbles, one by one.
'What if it gets too dark to see them?' asked Robbie.
 Robbie and Tamsin explored as far as they dared. The Wild Interior was full of
strange noises. Tamsin thought she saw a face looking at her from behind a tree.
'The Wild Interior doesn't like us being here,' said Tamsin, and they hurried back as fast
as they could, following the trail of white pebbles.

amsin and Robbie turned their backs on the Wild Interior, and ran races in the sand. They collected shells and watched rainbow fish darting in the shallows. Tamsin found a rose-red curly shell, as big as her fist. Robbie found an arrowhead.

At last evening came. Tamsin and Robbie were tired of eating golden apples, so they finished their bread and cheese. They lay down on their bracken beds, with Tamsin's blanket tucked over them, and fell asleep.

Robbie dreamed he was at home. His mum was washing the twins in the tub while Sam played with his toy boat. Mum said, 'There's jam roly-poly for tea.' Tamsin dreamed she was in her little bedroom with Demelza purring at her feet.

In the night the wind rose. It whipped up the waves and blew the hut door open. It tugged away the blanket and pulled the children's hair. Robbie and Tamsin woke up, and heard the roar of the storm. They were cold without their blanket, and frightened.
'I hope the hut won't fall down.'
'We'd better see what's happening.'

They went outside. The Wild Interior was surging in the wind. The sea was full of foam and wicked waves. The island didn't look like their secret island now.
'I wish Demelza was here,' said Tamsin.
'Tamsin!' shouted Robbie, 'Our boat is moving!'

The Islander's sails were filling with wind. She was going away without them.
'We'll be stuck here for ever!'
Already there was a gap between the boat and the jetty but they leaped across it, and tumbled into the bottom of The Islander. The wind blew harder and The Islander raced out out of the bay and over the stormy sea. Robbie and Tamsin held on tight as foam blew around them, and the little boat with red sails forged her way through waves like mountains.

D awn was breaking when The Islander sailed into harbour.
'Mum and Dad will be gone,' said Robbie sadly, 'We've been away a night and a
day and a whole night.'
The children climbed the harbour steps and slowly and wearily made their way up the
winding streets to Tamsin's cottage.

T amsin tapped at the door and it opened wide. There were Robbie's mum and dad, Sam, Sarah and Lucy. Tamsin's mum was cooking eggs and bacon.
'But why is everyone here, Mum?' asked Tamsin.
'You mazey-head, it's Saturday,' said her mum. 'They go home today. That's why we're up early.'
Robbie and Tamsin looked at each other. Saturday! In the town, only one night had passed.
'Have you been out for a last look at that island of yours?' asked Robbie's mum.
'Yes,' said Robbie.
Tamsin cuddled Demelza, who purred as if Tamsin had been gone for a long time. Maybe a night and a day and a whole night.
'Never mind, Tamsin,' said her mum, 'Robbie will be back next year.'

The train steamed away from the platform. Robbie waved and waved, and Tamsin stood on the platform waving back. Robbie held the arrowhead he had found. Tamsin held the rose-red curly shell, as big as her fist.

'Next year!' called Robbie.

'Next year!' called Tamsin.

In the far distance, a little boat was sailing away. There were dolphins leaping at its side, and its sails were red.

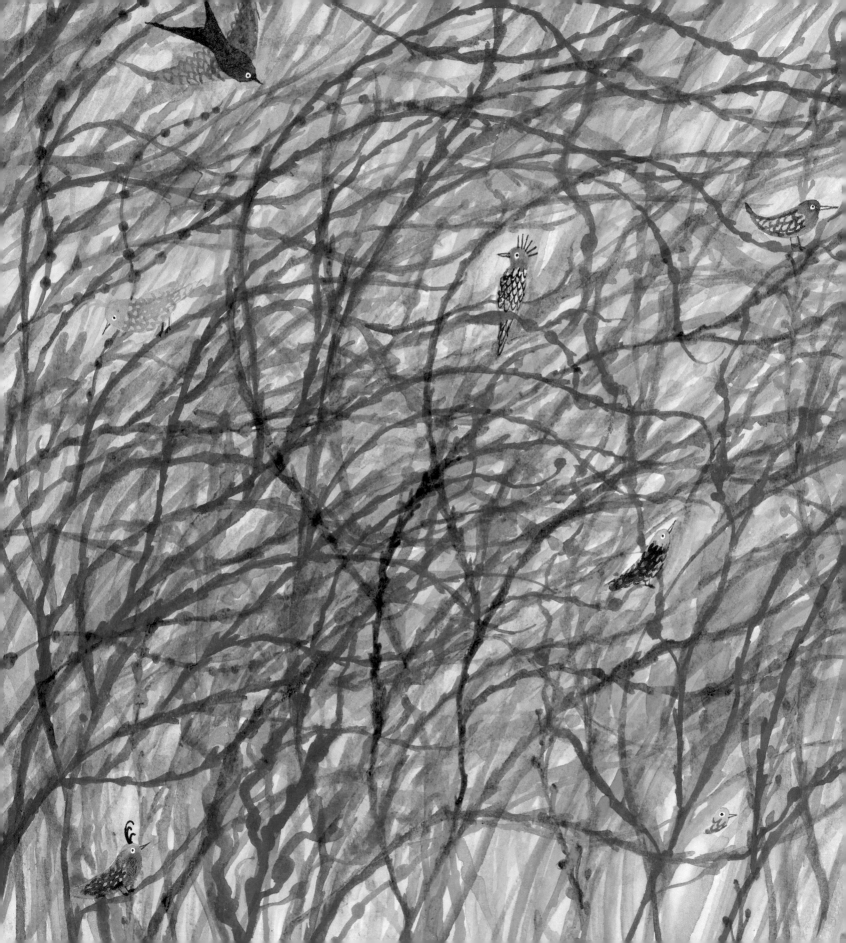